ASTRID & APOLLO

AND THE
BLAST FROM THE PAST

BY
V.T. BIDANIA

ILLUSTRATED BY
CÉSAR SAMANIEGO

PICTURE WINDOW BOOKS
a capstone imprint

To Ms. Loux's outstanding third grade class at McKinley Elementary —VTB

Published by Picture Window Books, an imprint of Capstone.
1710 Roe Crest Drive
North Mankato, Minnesota 56003
capstonepub.com

Text copyright © 2024 by V.T. Bidania.
Illustrations copyright © 2024 by Capstone.

All rights reserved. No part of this publication may be reproduced in whole or in part, or stored in a retrieval system, or transmitted in any form or by any means, electronic, mechanical, photocopying, recording, or otherwise, without written permission of the publisher.

Library of Congress Cataloging-in-Publication Data
Names: Bidania, V. T., author. | Samaniego, César, 1975- illustrator. | Bidania, V. T. Astrid & Apollo (Series)
Title: Astrid and Apollo and the blast from the past / by V.T. Bidania ; illustrated by César Samaniego.
Description: North Mankato, Minnesota : Picture Window Books, an imprint of Capstone, 2023. | Series: Astrid and Apollo | Audience: Ages 6 to 8. | Audience: Grades K-1. | Summary: A traveling museum is visiting their school and eight-year-old Hmong American twins Astrid and Apollo are among the visitors, but Astrid is apprehensive of things like mummies and dinosaurs—until she remembers her brother's advice.
Identifiers: LCCN 2022058410 (print) | LCCN 2022058411 (ebook) | ISBN 9781484675595 (hardcover) | ISBN 9781484675557 (paperback) | ISBN 9781484675564 (pdf) | ISBN 9781484675588 (epub)
Subjects: LCSH: Hmong American children—Juvenile fiction. | Twins—Juvenile fiction. | Siblings—Juvenile fiction. | Museum exhibits—Juvenile fiction. | Fear—Juvenile fiction. | CYAC: Hmong Americans—Fiction. | Twins—Fiction. | Siblings—Fiction. | Museum exhibits—Fiction. | Fear—Fiction. | LCGFT: Novels.
Classification: LCC PZ7.1.B5333 Ai 2023 (print) | LCC PZ7.1.B5333 (ebook) | DDC 813.6 [Fic]—dc23/eng/20221223
LC record available at https://lccn.loc.gov/2022058410
LC ebook record available at https://lccn.loc.gov/2022058411

Designer: Tracy Davies

Design Elements: Shutterstock/Ingo Menhard, 60, Shutterstock/Yangxiong (Hmong pattern), 5 and throughout

Table of Contents

Hi, I'm Astrid. My twin brother is Apollo, and we were born in Minnesota. We live here with our mom, dad, and little sister, Eliana.

ASTRID GAO NOU

Hi, I'm Apollo! Our mom and dad were both born in Laos. They came to the United States when they were very young and grew up here.

APOLLO NOU KOU

MOM, DAD, AND ELIANA GAO CHEE

HMONG WORDS

gao (GOW)—girl; it is often placed in front of a girl's name. Hmong spelling: *nkauj*

Gao Chee (GOW chee)—shiny girl. Hmong spelling: *Nkauj Ci*

Gao Hlee (GOW lee)—moon girl. Hmong spelling: *Nkauj Hli*

Gao Nou (GOW new)—sun girl. Hmong spelling: *Nkauj Hnub*

Hmong (MONG)—a group of people who came to the U.S. from Laos. Many Hmong from Laos now live in Minnesota. Hmong spelling: *Hmoob*

Nia Thy (nee-YAH thy)—grandmother on the mother's side. Hmong spelling: *Niam Tais*

Nou Kou (NEW koo)—star. Hmong spelling: *Hnub Qub*

pa dow (PA dah-oh)—needlework made of shapes like flowers, triangles, and swirls. Hmong spelling: *paj ntaub*

tou (TOO)—boy or son; it is often placed in front of a boy's name. Hmong spelling: *tub*

CHAPTER 1

Scary Storm

Astrid moved closer to her little sister, Eliana, on the couch. She lifted her hand up to her eyes, ready to cover them—just in case.

Apollo grinned. "Are you scared?"

Astrid nodded quickly. "This is a scary part!" she said.

The twins and Eliana sat in the dark living room, watching a movie about museum exhibits that came to life. Skeletons danced. Mummies roamed the halls. Prehistoric animals climbed out of their cases!

"It's not scary. It's exciting!" said Apollo.

Astrid shook her head. "It's scary to me!"

Eliana jumped up and pointed at the TV. "Scay-wee!" she said and giggled.

Even little Eliana wasn't as scared as Astrid.

Astrid hugged a pillow to her chest and peeked over the top of it. "This reminds me of that other movie we saw about the dinosaurs!" she said.

"You mean the one where the dinosaur chased those kids into the forest?" asked Apollo. He lifted his arms up high and wiggled his fingers, trying to scare Astrid even more.

A shiver ran up Astrid's back.

"Yes, that's the one!" she said. "Remember the dinosaur's loud footsteps that shook the ground?"

Apollo stood up. "Like this? Stomp . . . Stomp . . . Stomp!" He slowly stomped his feet on the floor.

Eliana giggled at Apollo and copied him. "Tomp! Tomp!" she cried.

All of a sudden, Dad jumped up from behind the couch and shouted, "BOO!"

All three kids screamed. Their little dog Luna barked and ran out of the room.

"What is going on?" Mom asked.

She came into the living room to see what all the noise was about. She turned on the lights, and everyone squinted at the sudden brightness.

Dad laughed. "I was playing with the kids."

"That wasn't funny, Dad." Astrid stood up and pouted.

"I thought it was kind of funny," said Apollo, chuckling.

"Me too!" said Eliana. "Boo!"

Astrid crossed her arms over her chest and frowned.

Dad leaned down and patted her shoulder. "I'm sorry, Gao Nou," he said. "I shouldn't have scared you. That wasn't nice. Can you forgive me?"

Astrid let out a sigh and shook her finger. "Okay, but no more scaring me."

"It's a deal," Dad said, and he gave Astrid a hug.

"Aww, but scary surprises are so fun," said Apollo, disappointed.

Mom turned off the TV. "All right, that's enough scariness for now."

"No!" all three kids said.

"The movie's not over yet, Mom!" said Apollo.

"You'll have to finish it later. Did you forget that tonight is the traveling natural history museum at school? Go get ready!" Mom said as she put Luna in her kennel.

"Oh yeah!" Apollo cheered.

"Oh yeah," Astrid said more quietly.

"Moo-zee-um!" Eliana shouted.

* * *

As they drove to the school, tiny drops of rain drizzled down. Astrid looked out the window. It was getting dark. She didn't like the dark. Especially after a scary movie.

Suddenly, lightning flashed in the sky.

"Look!" said Eliana, pointing. Everyone peered out as the drizzle turned into heavy rain. Then thunder boomed.

"This is spooky," said Astrid, sinking in her seat.

Dad turned on the car radio, and they listened to a weather report.

The rain poured down, making *thump-thump-thump* noises on the roof of the car while the wipers *swish-swish-swished.* Another flash of lightning lit up the sky.

"What a night to have a thunderstorm!" said Mom.

Astrid shuddered. It was dark *and s*tormy. Two things she didn't like.

CHAPTER 2

Ancient Artifacts

Dad pulled the car up to the school to drop off the family. Bright lights glowed from inside the building. Families were hurrying to the door, trying to dodge the rain.

Dad helped Eliana out of her car seat and then went to find a parking spot.

Mom was about to open an umbrella but changed her mind. "Let's just run for it, kids!" she said.

They pulled up the hoods of their rain jackets and hurried inside.

Inside the school, they got in line to buy tickets to the event. As they waited, Apollo noticed that Astrid still looked anxious. He had teased her earlier, but now he was feeling sorry about that. He asked Astrid if she was still scared.

Astrid nodded. "A little. You know I don't like the dark. And I keep thinking about that spooky part in the movie. All those creatures from the exhibits coming to life, moving and walking around!" Astrid shuddered.

"But it's not real. It's just a movie," Apollo said as they moved a few steps forward in line.

"It was still spooky!" Astrid insisted. A raindrop dripped from her hood, and she wiped it from her cheek.

Apollo wanted to help her, so he came up with an idea.

"How about this?" he said. "If something scares you, first ask, *is it real?* Once you remind yourself it's not real, you might not be as scared. Will you try that?"

Astrid shrugged. "Maybe."

"Second, tell yourself that you're brave and strong," said Apollo. He held up his arm to show his muscles.

"I am?" asked Astrid as she felt her own arm muscles.

"Of course you are! Think about all the brave and strong things you've done!" he said.

Astrid thought about it. Once she helped her family on a camping trip when a scary noise had frightened them. They told her she was very brave for doing that.

Another time she was in a tae kwon do competition, and even though she forgot what to do, she kept trying anyway. In the end, she won an award. Her teacher had said Astrid was strong because she hadn't given up.

"I guess," Astrid said, beginning to smile.

"I know you can do it!" Apollo said.

"Okay, I will . . ." Astrid was starting to feel a little better. "What's the third thing?"

"What do you mean?" asked Apollo.

"You said first and then second. Good things come in threes." Astrid tilted her head as she waited for his answer.

"Oh. Well, third is . . . I know— laugh about it!" Apollo said.

"That's a silly one, but okay. I'll laugh, and then maybe I won't be scared anymore," said Astrid. She checked her arm muscles again. "I feel braver already!"

"See, you *can* be brave! Maybe not as brave as me, but still brave," Apollo joked.

Astrid shook her head at him but giggled anyway.

Finally, they got to the front of the line where the principal, Mr. Kumar, was greeting the families. While Mom and Dad chatted with him, Astrid spotted some big boxes across from the drinking fountain. The boxes were labeled *Egypt, Cretaceous,* and *Tundra.* Astrid nudged Apollo and pointed at them.

Then they saw their classmates Oliver, Asher, Owen, and Auristella gathered together down the hall.

They were acting excited, chatting and bouncing up and down. Each time Oliver bounced, tiny lights flashed from his shoes. The lights were red, yellow, and blue.

"Look at Oliver's shoes!" Astrid said.

"Those would be great to have in the dark," Apollo replied.

Astrid agreed. She wished she had a pair of shoes that lit up. They could come in very handy.

"Astrid and Apollo, could you two please keep an eye on Eliana?" Mom asked as she hung up their wet raincoats. "We're going to catch up with some of the other parents."

"Come on, Eliana," Astrid said, holding out her hand.

The three of them entered the bright, noisy gym. Everywhere they looked were long tables and glass cases holding all kinds of amazing things. There were dioramas of wild animals, models of ancient footprints, and a huge nest full of giant bird eggs!

There was a feeling of excitement in the room. It made Astrid feel better to be around so many people. And the bright lights in the gym helped her forget about the dark and the scary movie.

They saw their friend Kiran with his family.

"Kiran, over here!" Apollo waved at him.

Kiran hurried over with a little boy. "Hi, Astrid and Apollo! This is my brother Ari. He's in kindergarten."

The twins said hello to Ari. He smiled at them, revealing that he already had two baby teeth missing.

"This is our little sister, Eliana," said Apollo.

Eliana gave a tiny, shy wave to Kiran and his brother. Ari waved back.

"Nice to meet you, Eliana," said Kiran. "Are you excited to see all the exhibits?"

Eliana nodded and then went to hide behind Astrid.

"I didn't know there would be so many cool things!" said Kiran.

Astrid pointed. "There are fossils and dinosaur bones over there!"

"And it looks like there are some ancient artifacts in those cases," Apollo said. "Maybe they're from the Ice Age!"

Eliana popped out from behind Astrid and pointed at a giant stuffed polar bear. It had sharp fangs and stood tall on its hind legs. "Bear!" she said.

"And a sabertooth!" Ari said, pointing at a stuffed tiger next to the bear.

Then Astrid saw a long, rectangular case in the center of the gym. There was a sign on it, but she couldn't read it from where they stood.

Apollo saw it too. "I wonder what's in that . . ."

Eliana pulled his arm. "Go see!" she said.

Ari took Eliana's hand and they rushed over to look.

"Wait for us!" Astrid said as she, Apollo, and Kiran chased after Ari and Eliana.

When they got there, Astrid was finally able to read the sign: SARCOPHAGUS.

She gulped.

CHAPTER 3

Flickering Lights

"I think I know what's in there," said Astrid. She took a step back.

Kiran nodded slowly. "Me too."

Eliana and Ari asked at the same time, "What is it?"

Luckily, just then, Mom and Dad spotted them and came over. "Kids, let's go sit down. The program is about to start," Mom said.

When everyone had found seats in the bleachers, a man at the front of the gym began speaking into a microphone.

"Welcome to the Traveling Natural History Museum!" he said. He was wearing khaki pants and a red vest. Next to him was a woman wearing a matching outfit.

"I'm Steve, and this is Trisha," he said. "We're your museum guides tonight."

Astrid and Apollo smiled at each other. Trisha and Steve looked like nice people who would share lots of cool facts with them.

"Steve and I are so excited to tell you about this wonderful collection," said Trisha. She pointed to the right. "On this side of the gym, you'll see displays from the Ice Age."

"That's what I said it was!" whispered Apollo.

Steve pointed to the left side of the gym. "And over here we have fossils and dinosaur bones."

Astrid smiled and nudged Apollo. "That's what *I* said!"

As Steve and Trisha talked about the Traveling Museum, lightning flashed through the windows. A second later, a loud clap of thunder boomed through the gym.

Eliana covered her ears. Ari went to sit with his mom and dad nearby.

"What a storm!" said Steve.

Trisha nodded. "Good thing we're cozy and dry in here!"

Then Steve said, "Later this evening, we have an exciting treat planned for you. Some special guests will blast here straight from the past!"

He and Trisha glanced at the doorway of the gym and chuckled.

Astrid, Apollo, and Kiran looked at each other curiously.

"Special guests from the past?" whispered Astrid.

"How will they *blast* here?" Apollo whispered back.

Kiran looked at them both and shrugged.

"But first," Trisha continued, "we're going to tell you about some of these amazing artifacts."

One by one, she and Steve held up different ancient and mysterious items. They showed metal jewelry, clay pots and vases, and tools made of stone. They told the audience where each artifact came from and how it was discovered.

During the presentation, another loud clap of thunder boomed. Kids screamed in surprise as the gym lights flickered off for a second, then came back on. Everyone sighed in relief.

Steve chuckled. "That wasn't part of our program, but this might be a good time for a brief intermission. Please have a look at the displays, and then in fifteen minutes, we'll bring out those special guests we promised!"

Eliana whined that she was hungry, so Mom passed around some rice crackers. They ate a few, but the crackers made them thirsty.

"Let's go to the water fountain," Apollo suggested to Astrid and Kiran.

Astrid turned to Dad. "Can Apollo and Kiran and I get a drink of water?"

"Sure," Dad replied. "But come right back so you don't miss the rest of the program."

The twins and Kiran hurried out to the hallway. As they passed the big boxes, Astrid noticed something. "Hey, they're open now! I wonder what was in them?"

"I don't know, but I'm thirsty!" Kiran said.

But when they got to the drinking fountain, they saw a sign taped over it.

"Out of order," said Apollo.

"There's another water fountain this way," said Kiran, pointing.

Astrid looked down the long hallway. During the school day, it was always filled with busy, noisy students. But now it was quiet and empty . . . and a little scary.

Brave and strong, Astrid reminded herself.

She took a deep breath. "Okay, let's go. I'm thirsty too!"

Astrid followed Apollo and Kiran to the end of the hall. When they got to the second water fountain, the lights flickered off again.

But this time, they didn't come back on.

CHAPTER 4

Is It Real?

Astrid gasped. She couldn't see anything around her. She couldn't even see Apollo and Kiran.

"The storm must have caused the power to go out!" Apollo whispered.

"Why are you whispering?" asked Kiran.

"I don't know!" Apollo said, his voice shaking.

Usually, he was the brave one, but right now, Apollo sounded afraid.

"What should we do?" he asked in the dark. "Where are you, Astrid?"

"I'm here," Astrid said, waving her hands in the air. She blinked several times, hoping her eyes would adjust. Soon she was able to make out the lumpy black shapes of Apollo and Kiran in front of her.

"Let's turn around and try to make our way back to the gym," she suggested.

"Turn which way? I can't see anything!" said Apollo in a panic. "What are we going to do?"

"Calm down," Kiran said. "It's okay."

"I don't like this!" Apollo wailed.

Astrid tried to move toward Apollo's voice, but she bumped straight into the drinking fountain instead. "Ouch!" she said, rubbing her hip. That's when she heard it.

It was soft at first. But slowly, it grew louder. And louder.

Kiran heard it too. "What is that?" he said.

"What's what?" asked Apollo nervously.

The noise sounded like shuffling feet. Someone, or something, was shuffling down the hall, and it was coming toward them.

Goose bumps spread across Astrid's arms. The shuffling continued.

"Is someone there?" Apollo said in a quiet voice.

Now they heard other noises. Was it talking? Or moaning?

It was growing even louder now. It sounded like muffled voices saying, "Help . . ."

Suddenly, Astrid saw a dark shadowy shape, like an arm sticking straight out. It looked spooky!

She remembered the case that read *sarcophagus*. That's where mummies lived! Astrid's heart pounded. Were the exhibits coming to life, just like in the movie?

Then, at the other end of the hallway, they heard it again.

"Help! Help ush . . ."

Another shadowy shape appeared. It was so close. It was almost in front of them!

Apollo screamed, "Run!"

Astrid and Kiran screamed too. The three of them ran farther down the dark hallway. They had to get away from the scary, shuffling shadows and spooky voices!

"Where are we going?" Astrid asked as they ran.

"Away from here!" shouted Kiran.

They spotted an open door.

"That room. Quick!" said Apollo.

The three of them dashed into the room. A flash of lightning lit it up. Astrid saw tables and chairs. At the front of the room was a big counter. She realized it was the science room—the creepiest of all classrooms in the dark. But it was the only open door.

"Let's hide here!" she said.

Apollo and Kiran followed her. They crouched behind a big counter. Astrid hugged her arms to her chest, trying to catch her breath. She could hear Apollo and Kiran panting.

Then came the shuffling sounds again. "Help . . . Help . . ." the muffled voices moaned.

Whatever was following them had found them.

In another flash of lightning, Astrid thought she saw . . . a mummy . . . and a dinosaur? She couldn't believe her eyes.

But Apollo had seen them too. "It's a mummy! And a T. rex!" he shrieked.

Kiran jumped up and bolted out of the room.

Astrid and Apollo ran after him, but they weren't sure which way he'd gone.

They ran down the hall, but it came to an end. There was nowhere left to run.

The sounds began again. This

time it was a scratching, scraping noise on the floor.

Astrid slowly turned around. She saw a huge, wobbly, dark blob. The blob lurched from side to side. In front of it was a long arm, or a tail? Or . . . was that a trunk?

"Help ush. We can't shee," moaned a strange voice.

Astrid started shaking. Apollo stood behind her, shaking too. She could tell that he was as scared as she was. She reached out and grabbed his hand.

"Help. Pleash help!"

In the flashes of lightning through the windows, Astrid could see the mummy and the T. rex from before. They were there now too, shuffling up behind the large blob with the trunk.

The wobbly, shaking blob came closer. It was so dark, but Astrid thought . . . could it be . . . *Was it a woolly mammoth?*

CHAPTER 5

Laugh About It!

Apollo had said, *first, ask yourself if it's real.* Second, *remember you're brave and strong.* Third, *laugh about it.*

Astrid couldn't laugh yet, but she knew a woolly mammoth couldn't really be standing in front of her. Neither could a mummy or a T. rex.

Not real, she told herself.

Then she reminded herself that she was brave and strong. *Brave and strong!*

She stared at the shadowy shapes and listened to their moans. As they lurched closer, Astrid noticed something. Beneath the mummy were tiny, flickering lights.

Red lights. Yellow lights. Little flashing blue lights. Astrid had seen those lights before. On shoes.

"Help!" Apollo screamed.

"STOP!" Astrid said in her bravest, strongest voice.

The shadows stopped. The shuffling stopped. The flickering lights stopped.

"Oliver, is that you?" Astrid said into the dark.

The mummy nodded its head. It was pulling at its neck, trying hard to take something off.

"We're shtuck!" the mummy said.

Astrid turned to Apollo. "It's our friends! They're in costumes!" she said.

But Apollo just stared at the shapes in the dark.

"It's okay," Astrid said. "Not real, remember?"

"We can't get out of this thing!" the front half of the woolly mammoth moaned. "Pull!"

"I'll pull this side. You get the other, okay?" Astrid said.

Apollo nodded. Astrid grabbed the shaggy head of the mammoth, and Apollo grabbed the back end. Together, they pulled and pulled until finally, the costume came apart and they landed on the floor. Each had one half of the two-piece costume in their hands.

Just then the ceiling lights flickered back on, and the hallway lit up.

Everyone blinked in surprise and looked around.

There were Owen and Asher, faces red and sweating from being stuck inside the woolly mammoth costume.

"What about me?" the T. rex moaned.

"Auristella!" Astrid said. She and Apollo worked to unstick the stuck zipper on her dinosaur suit.

"Thank you!" Auristella said. She climbed out of the costume and pulled the tiny claws off her hands. "You saved me!"

Finally, Astrid and Apollo turned to the mummy and helped unwrap his head.

Oliver flashed them a relieved smile, and the lights on his shoes flashed too.

"Thank you!" Oliver said. His face was as sweaty as Owen's and Asher's.

"You scared us!" Apollo said.

Astrid threw her arms up in the air. "Why were you wearing those things?"

Oliver wiped his forehead.

"Trisha and Steve needed volunteers," he explained. They helped us put these on and told us to wait for them at the end of the hallway, where no one would see us. But then the lights went out, and we got lost trying to find them!"

"We couldn't see anything!" said Asher.

"We tried to get out of the costumes, but we were stuck," said Owen.

Auristella nodded. "We heard your voices and hoped you'd help us. But you kept running away!"

Just then they heard more footsteps. Someone rounded the corner. It was Kiran!

He took one look at them and said, "What's going on here?"

* * *

When the group got back to the gym, they saw Trisha and Steve by the doors.

"I found them!" said Kiran.

"Where did you kids go?" asked Steve.

"We're sorry we lost you in the dark!" Trisha said. "We were on our way to get you when the lights went out."

"Who are they supposed to be?" asked Kiran, looking at the strange costumes his friends were holding.

"They're our special guests!" said Steve proudly. "Our Egyptian mummy, our woolly mammoth from the tundra, and our T. rex from the Cretaceous Period."

"Are you ready for your part of the presentation?" Trisha asked them.

"Sure!" Auristella said and began climbing back into her T. rex costume.

But Oliver, Asher, and Owen all shook their heads.

"I'm sorry, but I'm mummied out!" Oliver said. "I think I'm done for tonight."

Asher and Owen agreed and wiped more sweat from their brows.

Trisha nodded in understanding.

"So, sounds like I need to find three new volunteers . . ."

Steve smiled at Astrid, Apollo, and Kiran. "Do you three want to be our blasts from the past? They're only scary in the dark."

Kiran looked excited. "I'll do it!" Then he turned to Astrid and Apollo. "What about you?"

"Only if I can be the mummy!" Astrid said.

She and Apollo looked at each other and grinned. They knew what they had to do. They laughed!

- Hmong people first lived in southern China. Many of them moved to Southeast Asia in the 1800s. Some Hmong decided to stay in the country of Laos (pronounced *LAH-ohs*).

  LAOS

- In the 1950s, a war called the Vietnam War started in Southeast Asia. The United States joined this war. They asked the Hmong in Laos to help them. When the U.S. lost the war, Hmong people had to leave Laos.

- After 1975, many Hmong came to the U.S. as refugees. Refugees are people who escape from their country to find a new, safe place to live. Today, Minnesota is home to around 80,000 Hmong.

- Many Hmong American families enjoy outdoor activities like camping, boating, and fishing.

MAKE A MINI MUMMY!

What You Need

- craft sticks
- craft glue
- scissors
- cardstock or thin cardboard
- gauze or white tissue paper torn into strips
- black marker

What You Do

1. Create a body, arms, and legs from the craft sticks. You can cut the sticks in half to make the arms. Position the arms and legs at odd angles, or put both arms on one side of the body for a "zombie" position. Glue the sticks in place.

2. Cut a cardstock oval for the head and a longer oval for the torso. Glue them in place onto the sticks.

3. Once glue is dry, wrap the gauze or torn strips of paper like bandages around the mummy body and glue in place.

4. Draw a mouth and eyes on your mummy!

GLOSSARY

adjust (uhd-JUST)—to change or adapt

ancient (AYN-shunt)—from a long time ago

anxious (ANG-shuss)—feeling worried or uneasy

artifact (AR-tuh-fact)—an object used in the past that was made by people

Cretaceous (creh-TAY-shuss)—relating to the last period of the Mesozoic Era; the last era of dinosaurs

diorama (dye-or-AM-uh)—a three-dimensional model of a scene, often in miniature

exhibit (eg-ZIH-bit)—a display that shows something to the public

fossil (FAH-suhl)—the remains or traces of plants or animals that are preserved as rock

intermission (in-ter-MIH-shun)—a short break or rest during a performance or event

panic (PAN-ik)—sudden and extreme fright or worry

prehistoric (pre-hiss-TOR-ik)—from a time before history was recorded

sarcophagus (sar-KOFF-uh-gus)—a stone coffin; tomb where mummified bodies are kept

tundra (TUN-druh)—a cold area where trees do not grow

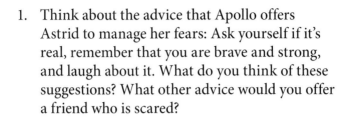

TALK ABOUT IT

1. Think about the advice that Apollo offers Astrid to manage her fears: Ask yourself if it's real, remember that you are brave and strong, and laugh about it. What do you think of these suggestions? What other advice would you offer a friend who is scared?

2. Sometimes fear can be important and help to keep us safe. Talk with a parent or caregiver about things that scare you and then come up with ways to stay safe when you're afraid.

WRITE IT DOWN

1. Can you think of a way to turn something scary into something funny, as Apollo suggests? Create a comic with two panels. In the first panel, draw something that is scary to you. In the second panel, draw the scary thing again, but add something funny. Perhaps a monster is wearing a silly hat? Or maybe a thunderstorm shoots rainbows across the sky instead of lightning! Be creative.

2. What do you think happened after the final scene in the story? Write a paragraph about Apollo, Astrid, Kiran, and Auristella as the "special guests" during the Blast from the Past presentation.

ABOUT THE AUTHOR

V.T. Bidania has been writing stories ever since she was five years old. She was born in Laos and grew up in St. Paul, Minnesota, right where Astrid and Apollo live! She has an MFA in creative writing from The New School and is a McKnight Writing Fellow. She lives outside of the Twin Cities and spends her free time reading all the books she can find, writing more stories, and playing with her family's sweet Morkie.

ABOUT THE ILLUSTRATOR

César Samaniego was born in Barcelona. He grew up with an artist father, smelling his father's oils, reading his comic books, and trying to paint over his father's illustrations! He attended Llotja Arts and Crafts School and graduated with honors in 2010. Since then César has published many books and provided art for apps, textbooks, and animations. He lives in Canet de Mar, a small town on the coast of Barcelona, with his wife, daughter, five cats, and a crazy dog.